THE GRE[Y]

CW00950175

This book is due for return on or before the last date shown below.

SCHOOL LIBRARY

Titles in Teen Reads:

Copy Cat
TOMMY DONBAVAND

Fair Game
ALAN DURANT

Mama Barkfingers
CAVAN SCOTT

Dead Scared
TOMMY DONBAVAND

Jigsaw Lady
TONY LEE

Pest Control
CAVAN SCOTT

Just Bite
TOMMY DONBAVAND

Mister Scratch
TONY LEE

The Hunted
CAVAN SCOTT

Home
TOMMY DONBAVAND

Stalker
TONY LEE

The Changeling
CAVAN SCOTT

Kidnap
TOMMY DONBAVAND

Dawn of the Daves
TIM COLLINS

Nightmare
ANN EVANS

Ward 13
TOMMY DONBAVAND

Joke Shop
TIM COLLINS

Sitting Target
JOHN TOWNSEND

Deadly Mission
MARK WRIGHT

The Locals
TIM COLLINS

**Snow White,
Black Heart**
JACQUELINE RAYNER

Ghost Bell
MARK WRIGHT

Troll
TIM COLLINS

The Wishing Doll
BEVERLY SANFORD

The Corridor
MARK WRIGHT

Insectoids
ROGER HURN

Underworld
SIMON CHESHIRE

Death Road
JON MAYHEW

Billy Button
CAVAN SCOTT

**World
Without Words**
JONNY ZUCKER

Badger Publishing Limited, Oldmedow Road, Hardwick Industrial Estate, King's Lynn PE30 4JJ
Telephone: 01438 791037

www.badgerlearning.co.uk

DAWN OF
THE DAVES

TIM COLLINS

Dawn of the Daves ISBN 978-1-78147-809-7

Text © Tim Collins 2014
Complete work © Badger Publishing Limited 2014

Publisher: Susan Ross
Senior Editor: Danny Pearson
Publishing Assistant: Claire Morgan
Copyeditor: Cheryl Lanyon
Designer: Bigtop Design Ltd
Printed by Bell and Bain Ltd, Glasgow

2 4 6 8 10 9 7 5 3

CHAPTER 1

DAVE ARRIVES

First there was just one Dave. Then there were loads of them.

Dave joined our class because his family had just moved to town. Or so he said.

He had blue eyes and blond hair parted on the right, so the left side flopped down over his forehead. His mouth was fixed in a grin. It never budged. He could have gone under a bus and crawled out smiling.

Dave made a lot of mistakes when he started here. Things you just don't do when you start at a new school.

Mistake number one: he was wearing a school blazer.

Blazers are an official part of our uniform, but no one ever, ever wears them. Sometimes a well-meaning aunt or uncle will buy one as a birthday present. And some poor guy will put up with the taunts of 'blazer boy' or 'blazer girl' for a couple of days before shoving it in the back of their wardrobe forever.

It's like coming in with a briefcase instead of a rucksack. You don't do it.

Mistake number two: he sat at the front of the class.

No one sits at the front. The cool gang sit at the back, then there's the moshers, then there's the rest of us, then there's an empty row of chairs at the front. Everyone knows that.

Mistake number three: he answered every single question Mr Baxter asked.

Let me get this straight. I have nothing against people who know stuff. I know stuff. My best friend Sarah knows stuff. But you don't join a new school and get every question right on your first day. That's asking for a bogwashing.

Bogwashing is the word for shoving someone's head down the toilet and flushing it, by the way. I'm pretty sure it's never actually happened. It's just a myth that gets passed on from one year of pupils to the next. But that doesn't stop me living in fear of a strong grip on the back of my neck every time I'm having a tinkle.

Anyway, no one gave Dave a bogwashing after that lesson. They didn't even tease him. They all crowded round to try and make friends with him, in fact. It was so strange.

I should have known something was wrong when Jade and Kieran from the cool gang sat next to him at the front of the class the next day.

It was all very weird. Not as weird as what was to come, of course. But nothing could be.

Sarah was the only other person who didn't fall under his spell.

"There's something wrong with him, Andy" she said to me. "His eyes are blank, like there's nothing behind them."

"That shouldn't make him stand out around here," I said.

"I don't mean he's stupid," said Sarah, "just kind of… plastic."

I knew what she meant. Although Dave's mouth was always fixed in a grin, his eyes were cold and distant. He was like a bad actor playing the part of a pupil.

If I'd known what he really was, I'd have run out of the classroom, down the stairwell, out of the playground, and kept running until I was miles and miles away.

CHAPTER 2

THE MEETING

"Another one?" asked Sarah. "This is getting silly now."

Until yesterday, Jay had been in the cool gang. His dark brown hair had been combed forward. Now he'd dyed it blond and parted it at the side. He'd worn a black zip-up hoody over his shirt. Now he was wearing a blazer. His mouth had been set in a permanent sneer. Now he was grinning.

He sat down at the front, next to the other Daves.

That's what we called them – the Daves. One by one, everyone was turning up in blazers, with floppy hair and fixed grins.

It wasn't just the boys. Caroline used to be the best-looking girl in the class. But one morning she came in with her long, blond hair cut short and parted at the side. I stopped fancying her instantly.

A new Dave clone walked in.

"Is that Craig?" asked Sarah.

"It can't be," I said.

But it was.

Craig had been a mosher. Until the day before, he'd had long, greasy hair, a black coat, and metal studs in his nose and ears. Now the studs were gone, he was wearing a blazer and his hair had been washed, dyed blond and styled into a Dave cut.

He was also smiling. It was so bizarre. He only used to smile on Halloween.

He sat on the second row, the nearest he could get to Dave.

At least there was no chance of Sarah turning into a Dave. She was always fussing over her long, curly, red hair. There was no way she was going to chop that off. And she loved the thick grey coat her gran had got her for Christmas, so I knew she'd never join the blazer brigade.

Mr Baxter strolled in and shoved his glasses up the bridge of his nose.

"Nice to see so many of you looking smart," he said, unzipping his fleece and throwing it onto his chair. "As I'm sure you're aware, Friday is the deadline for your Second World War coursework and I don't want any excuses."

The Daves stuck their hands up. They were all holding neat essays in clear plastic folders.

Mr Baxter leaped back as if they were waving poisonous snakes.

"Oh," he said. "Well done, guys."

It was like this all the time. Every hand would go up whenever a teacher asked a question. No one would ever tut, lean back on their chair or complain that the lesson was pointless.

Every break, the Daves would surround their floppy-haired god in the playground. The fan club grew and grew. First it was our class, then it was the whole of year eleven. Soon the rest of the school joined in, too, with year sevens milling around in tiny new blazers, desperate to get near Dave.

But even that wasn't as weird as what happened after school.

We were making our way to the bus stop when we passed a massive queue outside the gym.

"What are you waiting for?" asked Sarah.

Four of the Daves turned to us and spoke at once. "The debating club."

I wouldn't have thought anyone from our school was interested in debating. Unless you count arguing about who farted in assembly.

"Sounds interesting," said Sarah, joining the back of the queue. When we reached the door, we saw Dave standing inside. He tried to close the door, but I shoved my foot forwards.

"We're here for the debating club," I said, peering through the narrow gap. From what I could see, everyone was standing in neat rows.

"You wouldn't like it," he said, a grin still fixed on his face. "I don't think you'd fit in."

I took my foot away and the door slammed shut.

"Fit in?" asked Sarah. "You have to be a Dave just to take part? What sort of debate is that?"

As we trudged away, I heard voices from inside the gym. It didn't sound much like they were debating. It sounded more like they were chanting.

CHAPTER 3

THE PLAN

"I'm sorry Dave won't let you join his little club, Andy" Mr Baxter said. "But it's hardly my problem."

We were in the History classroom the following lunchtime. Mr Baxter was sitting behind his desk and grinning at the stack of coursework folders.

"They were up to something strange," I said. "I could hear chanting."

Mr Baxter looked up. "And how did that harm you?"

I wondered if I should pretend Dave had bogwashed me.

"Don't you think there's something weird about him?" asked Sarah.

Mr Baxter tapped the stack of plastic folders.

"Do I think it's weird that he's made everyone interested in learning for once?" he asked. "That over half my class are heading for A star grades? Of course I do. Am I complaining? No."

"You'd complain if you went to his debating club," I said. "There's something really freaky going on there."

"Dave doesn't want any teachers there," said Mr Baxter. "He told Mr McGregor."

"And you take your orders from that spod, do you?" asked Sarah.

"Of course not," said Mr Baxter. "Don't be silly." He was gazing down at the folders and grinning again. You'd have thought they contained wads of twenty-pound notes from the way he was looking at them.

We stepped out into the corridor. Bright sun was streaming in through the dirty windows. Sarah took her hairspray out of her coat pocket and gave herself a quick blast, so I ducked aside.

A couple of Dave clones walked past in spotless blazers. One of them was a girl I used to quite fancy, called Simone. Her black hair had always been in neat, thick braids. Now she had straight blond extensions, parted on the right and flopping down over her forehead.

Simone smiled at me. A couple of weeks ago, that would have given me butterflies. But this was a Dave smile, with no warmth in it.

"The teachers aren't going to be any help," said Sarah. "If we want to know what's going on in that gym we'll have to find out for ourselves. Let's hide in the equipment room and see what Dave's really up to."

"What if he finds us?" I asked.

"So what?" said Sarah. "He couldn't hate us more than he already does."

I nodded, though I wasn't sure. Something told me Dave could hate us a lot more than he already did. And that we wouldn't be safe if he did.

CHAPTER 4

THE CHANT

"Andy, he's here!" hissed Sarah.

She ducked away from the keyhole and I watched Dave stride into the empty gym. Even alone he had that same cold grin.

He stood at the front, facing the doors. Not looking at his phone, not flipping through notes, just standing there with his mouth fixed into a smirk. Weirdo.

Sarah nudged me out of the way, so I stepped aside.

By the time I took over at the keyhole again, the gym was filling up. The Daves were gathering in neat rows with their arms at their sides, like soldiers.

You'd never have been able to make that lot stand in complete silence a few days ago. They'd have been shouting, laughing, farting and pulling their jumpers up over their noses. What had happened?

Dave started speaking. But the sounds coming out of his mouth weren't like words at all.

"Tekeli- li! Tekeli-li!"

I was sure this would be too much for the other Daves. He'd gathered them all after school just to spout gibberish at them. They had to turn against him now.

But rather than jeering at Dave, the others joined in.

"Tekeli-li! Tekeli-li!"

"What's going on?" whispered Sarah.

"I think they're chanting," I said. I stepped aside to let her look.

"Told you he was weird," she whispered. "Record it."

I took my phone out and put the camera lens to the keyhole. I adjusted the angle until Dave and the chanting crowd could clearly be seen on the screen. I pressed record.

BEEP-BEEP! BEEP-BEEP!

Why did my Auntie Jean pick that moment to call? She must call me three times a year, max.

I peeped through the keyhole again and saw Dave striding towards us. I could feel my heart pounding.

"Sorry," I whispered. "I think he heard."

"I don't care," said Sarah, though her voice was unsteady. "Let's tell him what we really think about him."

The door flew open and Dave's grinning face appeared.

He beckoned us out and I skulked along the side of the gym. The grinning crowd were all staring right at me. Their bodies were facing forward, but their heads were slowly turning to track me.

"Sorry," I said, creeping towards the door.

As one, the crowd clenched their teeth and hissed. It was like someone had turned on all the Bunsen burners in the science lab.

"What's happened to you lot?" shouted Sarah.

I turned round. She was still just outside the equipment room.

"You should go," said all the pupils in perfect time. They sounded like they were reading a prayer in church. "You don't belong here. You don't fit in."

"You're right," I said, beckoning Sarah over to the door. "Our mistake."

"No it's not," said Sarah. She planted her hands on her hips. "Why are you acting like such a bunch of dweebs? Ooh, look at us, we're so cool with our blazers and our floppy hair. It's pathetic. What's happened to you?"

The crowd hissed again and Dave grabbed Sarah by the wrist. She let out a short cry as he dragged her towards the exit.

I'd like to say I jumped in and wrestled him away. But the truth is I ran straight out. It wasn't my finest moment. But that chanting was really freaky.

As I was getting my breath back I saw Dave shove Sarah out and slam the door.

I got a quick glimpse of his palm. I could have sworn it was covered with thick, white suckers like on squid tentacles.

CHAPTER 5

THE EVIDENCE

"Let's show Mr McGregor," said Sarah. "He'll have to admit it's weird."

We were sitting at the back of the library the following lunchtime. Sarah was rubbing her wrist, which was covered in sore, red circles where Dave had grabbed it.

We were watching the footage of Dave and his chanting disciples on my phone.

"It'll be the same as when we spoke to Mr Baxter," I said. "Brilliant grades, model students, blah blah blah. So what if they chant like devil

worshippers every evening? It's a small price
to pay."

"If Mr McGregor doesn't want to listen, we can
stick it on YouTube," said Sarah. "The whole
school will be closed down if it goes viral."

We crept out of the library. A group of Daves,
two male and two female, stared at us as we
passed.

We made our way down the corridor. Another
Dave was gazing at us from inside the music
room. I think it was Kieran Jones from year ten,
but it was hard to tell. They were all starting to
look alike with their blazers, floppy blond hair
and fixed grins.

We knocked on Mr McGregor's door. I'd never
been inside the headmaster's office before, which
made me even more nervous.

"Come in."

Mr McGregor was sitting behind his desk, wearing a tweed jacket and grey baseball cap. He was dunking a digestive biscuit into a cup of tea.

"How many times do I need to tell you lot?" he asked. "Make. An. Appointment."

"It's an emergency," I said. "About Dave."

Mr McGregor jolted forwards in his chair and dropped his biscuit into his tea. "He hasn't hurt himself has he?"

"No," said Sarah.

"Thank God for that!" said Mr McGregor, leaning back again. "Because I'm holding a special assembly tomorrow to appoint him as our first ever head boy."

I glanced at the notepad on Mr McGregor's desk. It contained nothing but the word 'Dave' written over and over again.

"There's something you should see first," I said. I selected the video on my phone, pressed play and handed it to him. "This is what really goes on at his so-called debating club."

Mr McGregor peered at the footage. I could hear the Daves chanting through the tinny speakers, "Tekeli-li! Tekeli-li!"

I was waiting for Mr McGregor to say something, but he just stared silently at the phone. When it finished, he tapped the screen and handed it back to me.

"So what did you think?" I asked. "Didn't you find it a little strange?"

"Find what strange?" asked Mr McGregor. "There was no video."

I looked at my phone. The video had gone.

"You deleted it!" I said.

"Don't speak to me like that," shouted Mr McGregor. "You can't just interrupt my precious lunch hour to spread gossip about my star pupil! Jealousy will get you nowhere."

He took off his baseball cap and his hair flopped down over his forehead.

My stomach lurched. Mr McGregor usually had wispy, grey hair. Now he'd dyed it blond and parted it on the right. He took off his tweed jacket to reveal a spotless school blazer, and a sly smile spread over his lips.

CHAPTER 6

THE TUNNEL

"You should get that looked at," I said.

We were sitting on the bench opposite the canteen, watching all the Daves file between afternoon lessons in neat lines. Sarah was scratching the red marks on her wrist. She'd broken the skin on one and there was a thin smear of blood trickling down her arm.

"It'll be fine with some cream," she said.

"I'm not sure," I said. "I know this sounds nuts, but I thought I saw suckers on Dave's palm when he dragged you from the gym."

"Suckers?" asked Sarah.

"Yeah," I said. "Sort of like on squid tentacles. Maybe I imagined it."

I thought Sarah was going to say I was as crazy as all the Daves, but she just stared at her wrist.

I saw one of the Daves break away from the line and make his way over to the bin shed at the back of the canteen.

No, this wasn't one of the Daves. This was the original Dave. The leader of the whole tribe.

I nudged Sarah and pointed at Dave as he crept into one of the shed's wide doors.

"That's where they put the rubbish, isn't it?" I asked.

The door slammed shut and Sarah leaped up.

"Let's have a word with him," she said. "While his little friends aren't around to stick up for him."

"Yeah," I said, "maybe."

I didn't like the idea of cornering Dave in the shed, but Sarah was already striding across the playground.

I could hardly let her go in alone. I jogged over and caught up with her as she was pulling the dusty, black door open.

The shed was a small, brick building that smelled of rotting leftovers. By the slanting light of the high windows I could see two rows of wheelie bins with a narrow gap down the middle.

"Dave?" I shouted. I lifted the lid of one of the bins, letting out a rancid smell that made me gag.

Sarah pushed her way down to the back and said, "Look at this."

There was a small hole in the floor. It looked as though it had been made by a powerful drill, and there were chunks of concrete around it. A dark tunnel slanted away underneath.

Sarah scrabbled down and shouted, "Dave?"

There was no reply.

I forced myself to follow her, lowering myself into the dark hole on shaking arms. A voice in the back of my mind was telling me to get out and run away. There was no way this could be safe.

CHAPTER 7

THE DISCOVERY

"There's a light up here," said Sarah.

We'd been crawling along for five minutes. God knows how deep underneath the school we were.

The tunnel widened and I got to my feet. Huge clumps of soil fell from my coat and trousers.

The passage opened into a huge chamber that curved to the right. Flickering light was throwing shadows around the corner. There were two figures, one large and one small.

I could hear Dave's voice. It became clearer as we inched along.

"Almost everyone is converted now," Dave was saying. "Just two left, a boy and a girl. But they'll be easy to take care of."

"Tekeli-li! Tekeli-li!" said another voice. It was so deep it shook loose soil from the tunnel ahead of us.

"There's a building called a hospital to the east," said Dave. "I'll turn my attention to it as soon as I've got rid of those two misfits. The humans will be very weak there."

"Tekeli-li! Tekeli-li!" said the deep voice.

I wanted to turn back. I didn't want to find out where that horrible, raspy voice was coming from.

But Sarah had other ideas.

She rushed around the corner and froze. Her mouth dropped open.

I forced myself to peer around the bend. A

wooden torch with a naked flame was rammed into the soil ahead of us. Beyond it was the thing Dave had been talking to.

The creature's base was a pulsing blob of green skin. Soft, white tentacle suckers were clustered over it, much larger than the ones I'd spotted on Dave's palm. Hairy spider legs stuck out on all sides.

Rising from the base were three long, thick necks with large, green faces on the end. They looked almost human, but had strange deformities. The first had bulging, lidless black eyes. The second was wonky, as if its jaw had been broken and set wrongly. And the third had a row of teeth as sharp as needles.

Sarah screamed and charged towards the monster, kicking one of its spindly legs.

"Tekeli-li," hissed the head with the sharp teeth. It swung a leg out and knocked her to the floor.

This time I didn't run away or cower in the corner. I dashed over to Sarah to try and help her. But I felt a strong grip on the back of my neck, and a sharp stinging pain spread along it.

I turned to see Dave grinning at me.

He shoved his other hand into my face. This time I could clearly make out the clusters of white tentacle suckers on his palm.

CHAPTER 8

THE FIGHT

The itch on the right side of my face was unbearable. I scratched my forehead, cheek and eyelid, but it only made it worse.

Dave swung at me again and I ducked aside. I knew I had to try and attack him, but I had no idea what to do. I'd never been in a proper fight before. I once kicked my cousin off the sofa for changing channels in the middle of Teletubbies, but that doesn't really count.

I curled my hand into a fist and punched Dave on the chin. He didn't budge. He didn't even stop smiling. My hand hurt, though.

Dave lashed his foot into my shin and I slammed back onto the muddy ground, knocking the wind out of myself.

Dave leaned over me and shoved his hand over my nose and mouth. It was like being smothered by nettles. I could feel clammy tentacle suckers pulsating between my lips and the smell of stale seawater filled my nose.

I heard Sarah screaming behind me and tried to turn. But Dave's firm hand held me down on the soil.

Dave knelt on my chest, forcing the air from my lungs. Bitter pain was filling my mouth and nose and I could feel my throat burning. Dave was still grinning. His annoying smirk was going to be the last thing I ever saw.

Sarah screamed again. There was a whooshing noise and another scream.

I wanted to know what was going on, but I was too weak to move. Dave was swimming in my field of vision as my breath ran out. I thought I could see two Daves, then three, then a whole crowd of them beaming down at me with their hair flopping back and forth.

This was the world I'd failed to prevent. Everyone, everywhere, turning into Dave clones so that horrible three-headed creature could crawl out of this hole and take over.

Everyone in the whole world was going to become a Dave. Mum, Dad, Auntie Jean, the Prime Minister, the Pope, Wayne Rooney, Beyoncé, Leonardo DiCaprio. All of them.

A weight flopped down on top of me, and my mouth and nose were free again. I gulped quick bursts of air.

I could still hear screaming behind me, but it was too deep and raspy to be Sarah. It was crying, "Tekeli-li!"

I looked around. Dave's lifeless body was on top of me, his hair flopping down over my chest.

I shoved him aside and forced myself up.

The monster was on fire. Thick smoke was filling the small cavern and there was a putrid barbeque smell. The creature was writhing around in the flames. Its singed legs were scrabbling against the earth and its three faces were thrashing wildly. The one with the lidless, black eyes yelped as black-green flesh bubbled from its face.

Sarah was standing next to it. In one hand she had the burning torch and in the other she had her can of hairspray. She held the can behind the torch and pressed the top, creating a powerful flamethrower.

A fresh wave of fire engulfed the head with the wonky mouth. It screamed like a cat under a truck. The head with the black eyes fell still and crashed to the ground.

Sarah blasted flames onto the head with the sharp teeth. It snapped at her before collapsing back into the body.

The spidery legs went into spasm and the creature let out a strangled cry of "Tekeli-li! Tekeli-li!"

It fell still.

I stared at Sarah as she got her breath back.

"Thanks for your help," she said, putting her hairspray back in her coat pocket. "It's not like I was in danger or anything."

"I was fighting him," I said. I pointed behind me, but Dave's body had gone.

I turned to see him striding towards me.

CHAPTER 9

DAVE LEAVES

I scrabbled to the top of the tunnel and pulled myself up into the bin shed. I took a deep breath. It was horrible, but it was also wonderful. Even the rotten stink of the bin shed was a relief after that smoky tunnel.

I crouched over the hole and helped Sarah get out. Then I helped Dave get out.

"It's coming back to me now," he said. "I was walking past the school when I felt the urge to come into this shed and go down this tunnel. I tried to resist it, but something pulled me in."

Dave wasn't smiling anymore. He was looking down at his hands. The white tentacle suckers were gone, leaving smooth, but filthy, palms.

"How long was I gone for?" asked Dave. "A couple of hours?"

Sarah looked at me and laughed.

"You don't remember any of it?" I asked. "Joining our class? Making new friends? Chucking us out of the debating club?"

Dave shook his head. After spending the last couple of weeks hating him, I felt sorry for him now. The creature had used him to take over the minds of everyone else. He'd been just as much a victim as them.

I limped out of the door and into bright daylight.

Mr McGregor was passing the canteen. He spotted us and ran over.

"What were you doing in there?" he asked, glaring at Sarah and me like we'd just spat in his tea. "Why are you covered in mud?"

"I don't know," I said. "Why are you wearing a school blazer? And what's with the hairstyle?"

Mr McGregor looked down at his sleeves and felt the top of his head. He caught sight of Dave and gazed at him in confusion.

"Who are you?" he asked.

Just a few hours ago, Mr McGregor had been planning to make Dave the school's first ever head boy. Now he had no idea who he was. I was quite relieved, really. If Mr McGregor couldn't remember any of it, then neither would anyone else.

"Nobody," said Dave.

He wandered out through the gates, and that was the last I ever saw of him.

THE END